Missy, the Mister

One Chick's Journey to Living a Marvelous Life

Elizabeth Chennamchetty

ILLUSTRATIONS BY
Katherine Gutkovskiy

E C
PRESS

PUBLISHED BY EC PRESS
ElizabethChennamchetty.com

Book Design by Monkey C Media.
MonkeyCMedia.com
Layout Revision: Jodi Giddings

Printed in the United States of America

ISBN: 978-0-9983615-5-0

Library of Congress Control Number: 2019903998

50% of the profits from the sale of *Missy, the Mister*
will be donated to The Gentle Barn.

For Michael

A teacher, a farmer, a friend, an incredible person.
We are so lucky you are part of our adventure.

And Mister

One marvelous rooster.

My name is Missy. I'm a sweet little chick.
This is my story. It isn't a trick.
I hatched from my egg in a warm incubator,
covered in goop, then moved one day later.
Placed in a bin, on a shelf, in a room,
I lived with chicks who knew how to zoom—
around and around a first-grade classroom.

You'd think that my story—how I came to be—
would be quite enough for one family.
But you just won't believe what I've seen.
I'll lay it all out—you'll see what I mean.

After 21 days in my little egg home,
I pecked…and I pecked…eager to roam.
My egg-tooth finally broke through the shell.
I wasn't so sure I'd make it out well.

I worked for hours. My birth was no joke.
Wet and tired, I lay there—gone was my yolk.
Impressive you say? Oh believe me, I know!
But hold up—my story is just starting to flow.

Students eagerly peeked in my bin for a visit.
Their voices excited to view the exhibit.
Michael, the teacher, made sure the kids knew
how to behave around baby chicks too.
He helped kid paparazzi stay mellow and calm
and made sure our bin kept us healthy and strong.

We spent our days chirping and walking around,
keeping warm in the bin with a wood-chip ground.
We ate our food, growing strong and tough,
but Michael decided that wasn't enough.
"Fresh air is what would be nice for these chicks!
Let's go outside—find a good spot to pick."

Out of the classroom and onto the field,
we had no idea that we might need a shield.
Kids sat in a circle—criss cross applesauce.
A few even stood to show me the floss.

When a few minutes quickly had passed,
someone looked up—a shadow was cast.
A voice said, "Oh no! Look! An attack!"
A hawk swooped in for a quick little snack.
I started to think, "Let's call it a day."
But Michael, the teacher, shooed it away.

It didn't take long—the excitement was gone.
We settled back down and the playdate was done.
We gently were placed back into our bin
and set on the shelf in the room we lived in.

Students would visit day after day,
eagerly peering at us the same way.
One of the kids seemed really intrigued.
He wanted to hold me and help me succeed.
He decided he wanted his very own bird—
told his family this chick is what he preferred.

His parents said it was okay with them.
So the family asked Michael for this special hen.
Three in all, they decided. One for each child,
to live in their house, where it's loud and wild.

Michael sent me to their house with two others.

They wanted three sisters…and not any brothers.

We were named Chickie-the-Chick-Chick, Missy and Brave.

They taught us about love and how to behave.

We were growing fast, but were still much too small,

so we lived in their house till we grew big and tall.

Mom finally decided we'd move to our coop.
She said, "I think it is time to regroup.
They can peck and climb, and play in their pen,
explore, spread their wings—these three little hens."

We were happy in there, with room to grow,
huddled together—we were buddies, you know.
We'd explore the yard, eat treats together,
search for bugs, and grow great big feathers.

One day really early, as the sun rose bright,
I decided to climb a big branch with some height.
My body felt proud and I wanted to sing.
A beautiful song made me feel like a king.

The people inside heard my beautiful song,
looked through the window and said, "Something is wrong!"
Their faces were worried—they looked at each other.
I could tell they were thinking, "This is a BROTHER!"

I sat on my perch and started to think,
"But I love to sing. If I can't, that will stink.
I don't want to lay eggs. I can't. It's not me.
A rooster is what I want to be."

Mom sent a message to Michael, the teacher.
It said, "Help, oh help, we might have a preacher!
If he sings in the morning, the neighbors will say,
'Not in the city! Make him go far, far away.'"

"I'll take him," said Michael. "You don't need a preacher.
It's no problem at all." (He's a very kind teacher.)

Together the family walked outside
and told me the news. I almost cried.
"Missy, I mean Mister…you are part of our family.
We need to make sure you are safe and live happily.
You love to sing songs. That can't happen here.
You need Michael's farm. That much is clear."

The next day I rode in the car to the farm.
I knew right away they would do me no harm.
"It feels cozy and warm here. This is my home.
They know my language and I'm free to roam."

Exploring the farmland, I waddle around.
I see all the animals and the new ground.
It's exciting to be here—but wait, what's that?
Hmm, looks like these farmers have a really sweet flat.

I think I'll go inside—have a look—meander.
I'll let them know what I think with some candor.
Wow! It's nice in here. If I have my way,
inside this house is where I will stay.

Now, to convince them…"I'm sweet as can be.
I have a good nature—you will soon see.
I can totally hang here and watch your TV,
and I'll sing with the sunrise if you'll let me.

This is the place I am meant to be.
My new dads really, really…REALLY like me."
But now it appears I have two little problems.
I'm not really sure how I can solve 'em.

There is an old dog. He seems calm and cool.
But inside his mouth, there's big teeth and drool.
 If I'm out and about and the dog is near…
what could go wrong? I know what I fear.

My new dads were able to set a safe mood.
I'm not left alone, so I won't become food.
I have a new pen for when they are away
We've been told, "No playdates during the day."

What is my second big problem, you wonder?
I'll give you a clue. It happens down under.
I'll call it a potty issue…you see,
I can't control my poop…or my pee.
It comes out wherever—a mess galore.
I can't stay in the house if I poop on the floor.

Lucky for me, I'm out of the bind.
They got me diapers…for my behind.
The diapers are eco-friendly, they say.
Stick them in the laundry—poop washes away.
Now I can strut my stuff with ease.
I won't wreck the furniture or spread a disease.

So now I can live in the house and just sing
and feel what it's like to live like a king.
I am happy and healthy and can be who I am.
I'm Mister…the rooster…with a marvelous plan.

KEEP CALM
      AND
           CROW ON

SOME OF MISTER'S FAVORITE FRIENDS

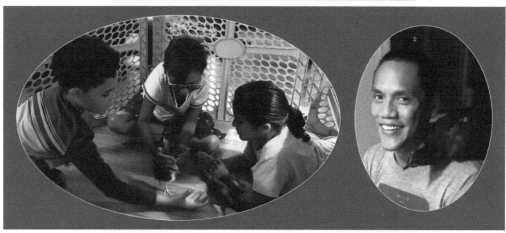

Mister, the rooster

Mister is a rooster living a marvelous life in sunny southern California with his humans and many animal friends. When Mister isn't strutting his stuff around the house, you can find him following his dads around the farm.

Michael, the teacher

Michael is a first and second grade public school teacher in San Diego, California. When he isn't teaching, you can find him at his ranch, tending to his many animals – spreading joy one goat at a time.

Elizabeth, the author

Elizabeth is a mom, author and blogger living in San Diego, California. When she isn't writing, you can find her out and about with her kids, using her graduate degree to complete enormous mounds of laundry and cook wholesome meals for her impossibly picky eaters.

Katherine, the illustrator

Kathrine is a mom of two wonderful boys and an illustrator living in Los Alamos, NM. When she isn't illustrating, she enjoys spending time with her family and teaching art classes for kids. She also enjoys traveling, which provides relaxation and inspiration for new projects.

COMING SOON!
Summer 2019

Mister
Nature, Nurture
& Teenage Trouble

9 780998 361550